GET THE GIGGLES WITH

YUCK

by Matt and Dave

Join Yuck's fanclub at

FOR SANTA'S HELPERS:

Bohanan   Tyler

Pedro   You   Cala

Jazz   Megan   Max

Camila   Samuel

SIMON AND SCHUSTER

First published in Great Britain in 2010
by Simon & Schuster UK Ltd
A CBS COMPANY
1st Floor, 222 Gray's Inn Road, London WC1X 8HB

1 3 5 7 9 10 8 6 4 2

A CIP catalogue record for this book is
available from the British Library

ISBN 978-1-84738-766-0

Printed and bound in Great Britain by
Cox & Wyman Ltd Reading Berkshire

www.simonandschuster.co.uk
www.yuckweb.com

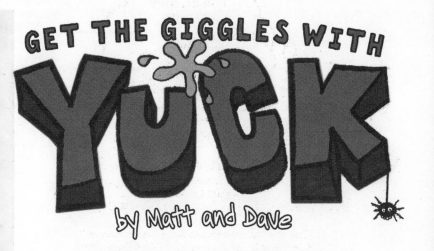

GET THE GIGGLES WITH YUCK

by Matt and Dave

YUCK'S CRAZY CHRISTMAS

AND

YUCK'S NAUGHTY NEW YEAR

Illustrated by Nigel Baines

YUCK'S CRAZY CHRISTMAS

Yuck unwrapped the golden foil from a chocolate coin. He popped the chocolate into his mouth and felt it melt over his tongue. Mmmm, I love chocolate! All morning, Yuck had done nothing but eat chocolate coins, one after the other, and golden foil wrappers lay strewn all over his bed.

Suddenly, Yuck's bedroom door burst
open and his sister Polly Princess walked in.
"Yuck, Mum says it's time to write our
letters to Father Christmas," she said.

"Polly, can't you see I'm busy?" Yuck
replied, unwrapping another chocolate coin.

"Hey, you're not allowed to eat those now!" Polly said. "Those chocolate coins are for putting around the Christmas tree."

"But they're yummy," Yuck said, smiling. He popped the chocolate coin into his mouth then licked his lips.

"I'm telling," Polly said, and she stormed back downstairs.

A moment later, Yuck heard Mum call from the kitchen, "Yuck, get down here at once!"

Quickly, Yuck gathered together the empty wrappers from the chocolate coins. Then, from his wardrobe, he fetched a plastic bag containing his scabs collection – it was full of scabs he'd picked and kept all year. He refilled the wrappers, placing a big crusty scab into each, then took them downstairs to the kitchen. "Is something the matter, Mum?" he asked.

Mum frowned at Yuck. "Polly says you've eaten the chocolate coins that I bought to put around the Christmas tree!"

"I don't know what she's talking about," Yuck said, placing the scab-filled coins on the table.

8

"Hmmm," Mum said, seeing them. She glanced to Polly who was sitting at the kitchen table. "Polly, it's not nice trying to get your brother into trouble like that. He hasn't eaten them."

"But I saw him!" Polly said.

"You couldn't have!" Yuck said.

"I did!"

"Didn't!"

Polly stuck her tongue out at Yuck, and Yuck pulled an ugly face back.

"That's enough, both of you," Mum said. "From now until Christmas Day I want the two of you to be good. Remember – Father Christmas only brings presents to GOOD children."

Yuck saw that Polly was already writing her letter to Father Christmas to tell him what presents she wanted. He sat down beside her to see what she'd put:

Dear Father Christmas,
I've been very good all year and I want a necklace, a lipstick and a Donna Disco glitterball.
From Polly Princess

"I thought we were only allowed to ask for one present," Yuck said to her.

"I deserve LOTS of presents because I'm VERY GOOD," Polly said smugly.

Yuck thought for a moment about what he'd like. A new football? A worm farm? A snake-and-slide skateboard?

Yuck ran his tongue along his teeth, licking the chocolate that was stuck between them. Yum, he thought, deciding exactly what present he'd ask for – a NEVER-ENDING CHOCOLATE MAKER! It was a present he'd seen advertised in *OINK!* comic – a brilliant invention that could make an endless supply of chocolate.

11

Yuck wrote his letter to Father Christmas:

Dear Father Christmas,
I've been quite good this year –
well, I tried to be, but sometimes
I got into trouble, like when I put
a frog in Mum's bath, and when I
swapped Dad's handkerchief with a
pair of dirty underpants. But even
so, for Christmas, please may I
have a NEVER-ENDING CHOCOLATE
MAKER.
From Yuck
p.s. Do you ever get chocolate
in your beard?

Yuck folded his letter and slipped it into an envelope. He addressed it to **Father Christmas, The North Pole.**

Polly stood up. "Mum, I've written my letter to Father Christmas. Can I go and post it, please?"

"Yes, of course, Polly," Mum replied.

Polly turned to Yuck. "I'll post yours too if you want."

Yuck looked at Polly suspiciously. "You'd better not lose it," he said.

"Yuck, Polly's just being helpful," Mum told him. "Now say thank you. It's very kind of her."

"Thanks," Yuck muttered, as Polly took his letter and ran out of the house heading to the postbox at the end of the road.

While she was gone, Yuck went to his room to make a space for the NEVER-ENDING CHOCOLATE MAKER.

Yuck decided that when he was EMPEROR OF EVERYTHING, he would live in a huge chocolate palace with chocolate rooms and a chocolate bed with a chocolate pillow that he could nibble at night. And on Christmas Day, Polly would be dipped in a barrel of liquid chocolate then fed to the royal reindeer.

Meanwhile, at the postbox, Polly posted her letter into the slot. She looked at Yuck's letter and smiled slyly. Wouldn't it be a shame if Father Christmas didn't get Yuck's letter? she thought. She glanced around making sure that no one was watching, then she tore Yuck's letter in two and hid the pieces in her pocket.

Later that evening, Dad came home with a Christmas tree and stood it in a bucket in the living room.

"Bagsy I decorate it!" Polly said.

"Can I help too?" Yuck asked.

Dad looked surprised. "That's good of you to offer," he said. "You can decorate it together."

Dad fetched a box of Christmas decorations from the hall cupboard, then went to the kitchen to make a cup of tea.

As Yuck opened the decorations box, Polly pushed him aside. "Go away. I'm doing it on my own," she said, taking out some sparkling tinsel.

"Hey, Dad said we're to do it together," Yuck reminded her.

"Tough!" Polly said, and she hung the tinsel on the tree. "You'll only ruin it anyway."

Yuck watched as Polly hung a shiny bauble on too. Then he had an idea. Behind Polly's back, he picked some bogeys from his nose and rolled them together into a big green bogey bauble. He dropped it into the box of decorations.

When Polly took the bauble out, it squelched in her fingers. "Urgh!" she yelled. "This bauble's gooey!"

Yuck giggled, seeing it sticking to her hand as she tried to hang it on the tree.

"What would make this tree look really cool is some snow," Yuck said. "Here, let me help." Yuck shook his head, sending a blizzard of white flaky dandruff from his hair. It settled on the Christmas tree and on Polly.

"Yuck, no!" Polly cried. "You're disgusting!"

Yuck ran to the kitchen giggling. He
fetched the pile of scab-filled coins then
dashed back and handed them to Polly.
"Don't forget to put the chocolate coins
around the tree, Polly," he said.

Polly took them angrily and started
placing them at the base of the tree.

"Oh, and Mum said you're allowed to eat one now if you want," Yuck told her.

"Really?" Polly asked.

"Yes, because you've been so good."

"Mmm, I love chocolate coins." Polly unwrapped the golden foil from one and popped it into her mouth. She chewed. "URGH!"

"What's the matter, Polly?" Yuck asked innocently.

Polly spat and spluttered. "This isn't chocolate!" She peeled a big crusty scab from her tongue. "UUUURGH! Scabs!"

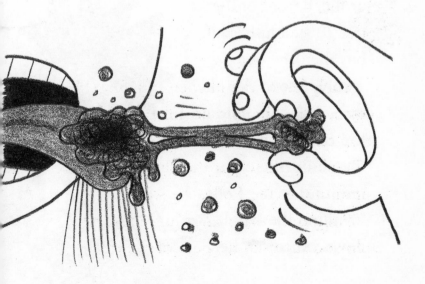

"Right, that's it, Yuck!" Polly said, pushing Yuck to the side of the room. "Move and I'll exterminate you."

Yuck stood giggling while she finished decorating the tree. He saw her take a plastic fairy from the box of decorations, then stand on a chair and reach up to put the fairy on the top of the tree. Yuck crept to the box of decorations and took out a Christmas cracker. He waited until Polly was at full stretch then pulled it: **BANG!**

"Eeek!" Polly screamed, startled by the noise. She wobbled and grabbed hold of the tree to steady herself, but then the tree wobbled too. "Aargh!" she cried, clutching its top and toppling from the chair. She came crashing to the floor, bringing the whole tree down on top of her.

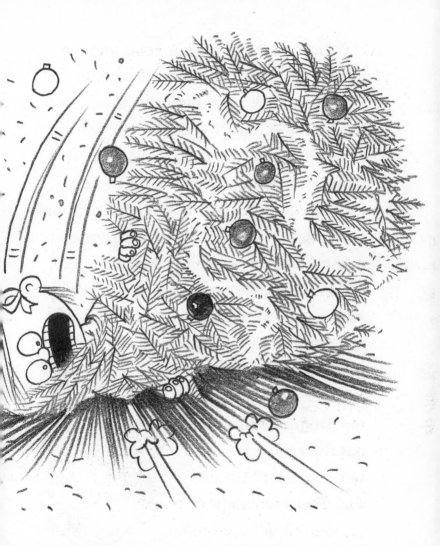

"Oh, Polly, now look what you've done,"
Yuck said. "Mum and Dad will be cross."
  Polly was crumpled under the tree,
wrapped in decorations. "I hate you, Yuck!"

All the next week, Yuck became more and more excited, looking forward to Christmas Day and the thought of getting a NEVER-ENDING CHOCOLATE MAKER. To make sure that Father Christmas brought him one, each day he tried his very best to be good. But it wasn't easy – whenever he tried to help with anything, Polly wouldn't let him.

When they were making Christmas cards together, Polly wouldn't share the felt-tip pens OR the glitter OR the glue.

"Polly, we're meant to be making them together," Yuck said.

"Tough," Polly replied. She'd already made four Christmas cards of her own: one of a reindeer, another of a glittering star, and two with pictures of herself.

"Can't I draw something?" Yuck asked, looking at his blank white card.

"No," Polly said meanly. She sniggered. "Why don't you pretend it's a snowstorm?"

As Polly started making a fifth card,

Yuck had an idea. He reached behind her back and sneaked the tube of glue from the table, then squeezed it under her bottom. "Your cards are great, Polly. Why don't you go and show them to Mum?" he said.

But when Polly tried to stand up, she couldn't. She was glued to the chair! "Eek, my bottom! My bottom's stuck!" she cried. "I hate you, Yuck!"

Later in the week, when Yuck and Polly were helping Mum make Christmas mince pies, Polly wouldn't let Yuck have any filling for his pie.

"Polly, my pie's empty," Yuck said.

"Tough. Mine's full to the brim," Polly replied. She marked her mince pie's pastry top with a letter P for Polly, then placed it on a baking tray ready to go in the oven.

Yuck had an idea. While Mum and Polly were putting the oven on, he sneaked to

 Furball the cat's food bowl and filled his mince pie with smelly cat food. Then

he took the pastry lid from Polly's pie and placed it on his cat-food pie instead. "Yum, I can't wait until these are ready," he said.

"Me too. Mince pies are my favourite," Polly replied.

Mum put them into the oven to bake.
But when the pies were cooked and Polly
bit into hers, her nose curled and her
mouth twisted. "Uuuuurgh!" she cried.

"What's the matter, Polly?" Yuck asked.
"Don't you like it?"

Polly spat out a mouthful of cat food.
"It's revolting! I hate you, Yuck!"

When Yuck and Polly went carol singing, Polly said Yuck's singing was so bad that he'd have to whistle instead.

Polly knocked on the door of a neighbour's house, and the old lady who lived there opened it. "Hello, we're singing carols for Christmas," Polly said to her. "Would you like to hear one?"

"Oh, yes please," the old lady replied.

But Yuck had secretly changed the words on Polly's songsheet. He whistled as she started singing:

"*Oh, Christmas tree,*
Oh, Christmas tree,
The old lady
smells of wee."

The old lady gasped and her false teeth flew out. "How dare you say that, you naughty little girl!"

Polly looked at her songsheet, confused. "Hang on, someone's changed this!" she said. Then she saw Yuck giggling beside her. "It was you, wasn't it? I hate you, Yuck!"

At school, in the Christmas play, Polly had the starring role of Cinderella, and Yuck had to be the back end of a pantomime horse that pulled her carriage. What's more, Fartin Martin was the front end of the horse, so Yuck had to hold his nose to keep from smelling Fartin Martin's blow-offs.

Half way through the play, Polly called from her carriage, "Take me to the Royal Ball, horsey!"

Yuck had an idea. Inside the horse costume, he whispered to Fartin Martin: "Start running in circles…"

The pantomime horse ran round and round the stage, sending Cinderella's carriage into a spin. Polly was tumbling around inside it. "No horsey! Bad horsey! Stop!" she called.

But Yuck and Fartin Martin galloped
faster, whizzing the carriage round and
round, making Polly dizzy.

"Help! I feel ill!" she cried.

Yuck and Fartin Martin suddenly
stopped running, and, as the coach came
to a halt, Polly tumbled from it onto the
stage. She tried to stand, her legs wobbling,
and threw up over the front
row of the audience.

"BLURGH! I hate
you, Yuck!"

At last it was Christmas Eve, and Yuck and Polly were hanging their stockings in the living room ready for Father Christmas to come down the chimney and deliver their presents. Polly's stocking was pink and very long – large enough for all the presents she'd asked for. Yuck's was a smelly old

football sock.

"Phwoar!" Polly said. "You're not hanging that next to mine, Yuck. It stinks!"

"So?"

"So I don't want my presents getting smelly. You'll have to put yours somewhere else."

"But Polly, that's not fair. Father Christmas might not find it."

"Tough!" Polly said, and she snatched Yuck's Christmas stocking and threw it out of the living room door.

As Yuck went to fetch it, he had an idea. He ran to his room to make Polly some special presents of his own.

Yuck picked a long string of snot from his nose and joined its ends like a necklace. Then he dug  his finger in his ear, pulling out lumps of earwax and rolling them together in the shape of  a lipstick. He wrapped both presents in shiny paper, then put on his red dressing-gown and stuck cotton-wool to his face like a beard to look like Father Christmas. "Ho, ho, ho!" he said, creeping back downstairs to the living room.

Polly looked round, shocked. "Father Christmas, is that you?" she asked.

"I couldn't fit down the chimney so your brother let me in," Yuck replied.

"But it's not Christmas Day until tomorrow. How come you're here already?"

"I thought I'd get an early start." Yuck slipped the two shiny presents into Polly's stocking.

Polly grabbed the presents and unwrapped them excitedly. "Wow! A necklace! Brilliant! And a lipstick!"

She put the necklace on and smeared the lipstick over her lips. She started spitting. "Urgh! This lipstick tastes of earwax!"

She felt the necklace sticking to her neck. "And this necklace is made of snot!"

Yuck was laughing. "Ho! Ho! Ho!" he said, pulling off his cotton-wool beard. "What's the matter, Polly? Don't you like your presents?"

"It's you, Yuck!" Polly screamed. "I hate you!"

Polly stamped her foot, fuming with anger. "Just you wait until tomorrow," she said. "You won't be laughing when the real Father Christmas brings me LOTS of presents and you get NONE."

"What do you mean?" Yuck asked. "I'm going to get a NEVER-ENDING CHOCOLATE MAKER."

"Oh, no, you're not!" Polly said. She reached into her trouser pocket and took out Yuck's torn-up letter to Father Christmas! "Oh dear. I forgot to post it."

Yuck stared in shock. "But—"

Polly threw the torn-up letter at him. "Merry Christmas, Yuck!" she said. And she ran upstairs to her room laughing.

Yuck couldn't believe how mean Polly had been. Now Father Christmas wouldn't know to bring him a present!

For the rest of the evening, Yuck paced up and down thinking what to do.

When everyone had gone to bed, he crept outside and, using Dad's ladder, climbed up to the roof of the house. It was cold, and there was snow on the rooftop. In large letters he wrote in the snow: **HELP**. Then he waited, looking up at the sky, hoping to see Father Christmas fly overhead on his sleigh.

Yuck waited for hours, shivering in his dressing-gown, snotcicles gathering on his nose. In the middle of the night, he heard the jingling sound of sleighbells and saw reindeers flying in the sky towing a sleigh.

The reindeer galloped down to the roof and landed beside Yuck. He saw Father Christmas on the sleigh surrounded by sacks of presents!

"Ho! Ho! Ho!" Father Christmas said to Yuck. "How nice of you to offer."

"To offer?" Yuck asked. "To offer what?"

"To offer me your help," Father Christmas replied, stepping out and pointing to the word **HELP** that Yuck had written in the snow on the rooftop.

"No, you don't understand," Yuck said. "It's about my pres—"

"I'm running late, you see," Father Christmas continued. "I could do with some help. I've only got a few hours to get all these presents delivered."

Yuck looked at the sacks full of presents on the sleigh.

"Will you help me deliver them? We can do it in half the time if we share the work," Father Christmas said. "My reindeer will carry us." He stepped along the line of eight reindeer.

"This is Dasher, Dancer, Prancer, Vixen, Comet, Cupid, Donner and Blitzen."

As Father Christmas was standing beside Dasher, the reindeer pulled a funny face. Yuck saw that it was doing a poo.

"Oh, not on the roof, Dasher!" Father Christmas said. From the back of the sleigh, he fetched a shovel and a plastic sack. "Mind you, it's even worse when they do it in mid-air and it lands on someone."

Father Christmas shovelled the reindeer poo into the plastic sack, then placed the sack on the back of the sleigh and sat in the front seat. "Are you coming?" he asked Yuck.

"Yes, please!" Yuck said, and he climbed aboard.

Father Christmas passed Yuck the reins. "Why don't you drive?" he said. "Just give them a tug and say 'Yee-ha!'"

Yuck tugged the reins. "Yee-ha!" he called, and the reindeer galloped along the

roof then took off into the air. The sleigh
whizzed through the sky in a sparkling
trail. It felt amazing!

Yuck and Father Christmas flew over towns and countryside, stopping at houses to deliver presents to the children who lived there. Father Christmas showed Yuck how to tiptoe across rooftops without being heard, how to climb down chimneys and even how to scoop up reindeer poo so no one knew they'd been.

"Right, that's most of this country done. Now to Germany," Father Christmas said.

"To Germany?" Yuck asked.

"Oh yes, we've still got half the world to do."

The reindeer went into turbo-trot, the sleigh whizzing around the world. From Spain to Siberia, America to Australia, Yuck and Father Christmas delivered more and more presents.

Gradually, the sacks of presents grew lighter, until at last there were no more presents to deliver.

They flew the sleigh high across the ocean then over fields and towns back to the roof of Yuck's house. As they arrived, dawn was beginning to break.

"We made it just in time, thanks to you," Father Christmas said.

"It was fun," Yuck replied, stepping off the sleigh.

As he did, Father Christmas reached under his seat. "Don't forget these," he said, handing Yuck two presents wrapped in shiny paper. One had a label saying **POLLY**. The other had a label saying **YUCK**.

Yuck had been so busy delivering everyone else's presents that he'd completely forgotten about his own! "But I didn't think you got my letter," he said.

Father Christmas winked. "I took a guess at what you might want."

"Thanks, Father Christmas!" Yuck
replied excitedly. He felt so happy. He'd got
a present after all!

"And if you're ever near the North Pole,
drop in and say hello," Father Christmas
told him.

Yuck smiled then climbed down inside
the chimney, heading indoors, excited to
open his present.

Yuck came out of the chimney into the living room. He put Polly's present into her stocking then, as he was about to tear the shiny paper from his own, he heard a voice say, "Stop right there." Yuck turned and saw Polly shining a torch from behind the sofa.

"You just put another trick present in my stocking, didn't you?" she said.

"No. It's a real one," Yuck replied. "I've been helping Father Christmas."

"Nonsense," Polly said. "I've waited up all night and Father Christmas hasn't been."

Polly took the present from her stocking.
"So what is it this time? Another snot
necklace? More earwax lipstick?"

"No, you don't understand. It really is
from Father Christmas," Yuck told her.

"I'm not falling for your tricks, Yuck,"
Polly said, and she threw the present at him.
It missed and hit the wall with a sMAsH!

"Oh dear," Yuck said.

Polly's present lay broken on the floor, its
wrapping paper torn and pieces of silver
glass spilling out.

"No!" Polly
cried, rushing to
it. It was the
Donna Disco
glitterball that
she'd asked for –
it was ruined!

"Wow, look what I've got!" Yuck said, unwrapping his present. It was a machine with a mixing bowl and a conveyor belt dispenser. Written on its side were the words NEVER-ENDING CHOCOLATE MAKER. "Rockits! It's just what I wanted!" he said excitedly.

"It's not fair!" Polly said. "My present's broken. I want another one!"

"Father Christmas has finished his deliveries now, Polly. He's just dropped me home."

"Where is he?" she said angrily. "I want a word with him!"

Polly raced outside in a huff. She looked up to the roof of the house where Father Christmas was about to take off in his sleigh. "Hey, stop this instant!" Polly called up.

Father Christmas looked down to see her.

"I demand another present!" she said.

Father Christmas shook the reins and flew the sleigh down to the garden. "Whatever's the matter, young lady?" he asked.

"The present you gave me is broken," Polly told him.

"Broken? How did that happen?" Father Christmas asked.

"Just give me another," Polly demanded. "In my letter I asked for LOTS."

"Oh yes. I remember. You must be Polly," Father Christmas said.

"Yes, Polly Princess."

"Well, I'm sorry, Polly Princess, but all the presents have gone now," Father Christmas told her. He glanced to the back of the sleigh at all the empty present sacks.

"What about that sack?" Polly asked, pointing to a black plastic sack at the far end. "That one looks full."

Father Christmas chuckled. "Oh, I don't think you'll want what's in there," he said.

"Yes I do! Give it to me!" Polly demanded. She dashed to the rear of the sleigh and leaned in trying to grab it.

At that moment, Yuck came outside. "Father Christmas, maybe you should let her have it," he said. "I think it's the perfect present for her."

"Yes, let me have it!" Polly shrieked.

"Very well. If you insist." Father Christmas shook the reins, and with a "Yee-ha!" the reindeer took off. The sleigh flew up steeply and the black sack tipped backwards, emptying a shower of reindeer poo onto Polly.

"Aaarrrgggghhh!" Polly cried, as the poo plopped down, covering her from head to toe.

"UUUUUUUUURRRGH!"

Reindeer poo stuck to her hair and ran down her pyjamas.

Mum and Dad came hurrying from the house wondering what all the noise was.

"Polly, Yuck, what are you doing out here?" Mum asked.

Dad pinched his nose. "Polly, why are you covered in poo?"

Polly pulled a lump of reindeer poo from her ear. "It was Yuck and Father Christmas!" she screamed. "I asked for a present, and all I got was pooed on."

Mum and Dad looked at Yuck who was laughing.

"Ho! Ho! Ho!" Yuck said. "Merry Christmas, Polly!"

YUCK'S NAUGHTY NEW YEAR

It was the first day of the new year and Yuck woke up excited. He picked a sticky bogey from his nose. Brilliant! A whole new year of bogeys! He put on a pair of smelly socks. Fantastic! A whole new year of toe cheese! He stroked a slug on his desk. Cool! A whole new year of slug slime! Yuck was going to have a whole new year of yucky fun!

"Yuck, are you awake yet?" Mum called from the kitchen.

"Yes, Mum," Yuck called back.

Yuck got dressed and headed downstairs to have breakfast. He saw Mum unpacking groceries with his sister, Polly Princess. "Happy New Year," he said to them cheerily.

Mum looked at her watch. "Yuck, you've slept half the morning!"

"Yuck, you're SO lazy," Polly said. "I'VE been up for hours helping Mum. It's one of my New Year's resolutions."

"What New Year's resolutions?" Yuck asked.

"These," Polly said, showing him a piece of paper on the kitchen table on which she'd written a list of promises:

I promise to clean my teeth.
I promise to have lots of baths.
I promise to do my homework.
I promise to help around the house.

What a goodie-goodie, Yuck thought.

"Well, Yuck, what are your New Year's resolutions?" Mum asked him.

Yuck thought for a moment. "Erm... er... I promise to have fun," he said.

"That's not a proper New Year's resolution, Yuck," Mum told him.

"Yes it is," Yuck said.

"No it isn't, Yuck," Polly interrupted. "A New Year's resolution is a promise to do something good."

Yuck decided that when he was EMPEROR OF EVERYTHING, everyone would have fun, all year long. It would be the LAW. People would promise to laugh and to party and Polly would be dunked in the sensible swamp and gobbled by the goodie-goodie gators.

Yuck pulled a box of Monster Snaps from the shopping and sat down to have his breakfast.

"Yuck, you're meant to be putting the shopping away, not eating it," Polly said.

"But I'm hungry," Yuck replied.

"Well don't eat too much, Yuck," Mum told him. "It'll soon be time for lunch."

Yuck began scoffing a bowlful of Monster Snaps, thinking what he could do that would be fun. "Mum, can we go to the park?" he asked.

"No, Yuck," Mum said.

"But it's fun at the park, Mum. I did just promise to have fun."

"I told you, Yuck, promising to have fun is not a proper New Year's resolution. There'll be no going to the park today – especially after what happened last year."

Yuck giggled, remembering what he'd got up to…

Last year, Yuck and Polly had gone to the park to take photographs of wildlife for a school project.

"I'm going to photograph a butterfly," Polly said.

"I'm going to photograph a monster," Yuck replied.

"Don't be silly, Yuck. There aren't monsters in the park." Polly switched on her camera and headed to the flower garden. But just as she found a butterfly to photograph, Yuck let out a **HOWL!**

Polly jumped, startled by the sound, and the butterfly flew away.

Yuck called to her, "I just heard a monster howl, Polly."

Polly looked round, annoyed. "That wasn't a monster, Yuck. That was you!" Then she glanced at the flower where the butterfly had been. "You ruined my photo."

Yuck giggled as Polly searched for

another butterfly to photograph, but just as she spotted one, he let out a loud **GRUNT!** Polly jumped, startled by the sound, and the butterfly flew away.

Yuck giggled. "I just heard the monster again, Polly," he called.

"That wasn't a monster, Yuck. That was you!" Polly replied, annoyed. "You ruined my photo again."

She searched for another butterfly to photograph, but just as she spotted one, Yuck let out a **ROAR!** Polly jumped, startled again, and the butterfly flew away.

"Right, Yuck, I've had enough!" Polly yelled angrily, and she chased Yuck across the park.

"But it really was a monster, Polly."

Yuck stopped by the park pond. "I saw it come this way. It must be a swamp monster."

"Don't be ridiculous," Polly said.

"I'm not. It was gnashing its teeth. In fact it was chasing a butterfly."

Yuck pointed up into the branches of a tree by the pond. "Look, the butterfly flew up there."

Polly looked up into the branches.

"It was a beautiful butterfly, Polly, with yellow spotted wings. You should take a photograph of it."

Polly's eyes lit up with excitement, and she began climbing the tree with her camera at the ready. "Where did the butterfly go? I can't see it," she said.

Yuck pointed to a long branch high above the pond. "It's there somewhere," he called up.

Polly crawled out along the branch.

"Keep going," Yuck told her. "All the way to the end."

But as Polly did, there was a loud **CRACK!** and the branch snapped. "Argh!" she yelled, falling into the pond with a **SPLASH!**

Yuck giggled as she stood up covered in pondweed. "Urgh!" she cried. "It's all stinky!"

Yuck pointed his camera and took a photograph. "Smile, Polly. You look just like a monster!"

In the kitchen Yuck giggled as he ate his breakfast. If he wasn't allowed to go to the park today, then what else could he do that was fun? he thought. "I know what, Mum!" he said, Monster Snaps spraying from his mouth. "Why don't we go swimming? That's fun too!"

"Yuck, I told you, having fun is not a proper New Year's resolution!" Mum said. "So there'll be no swimming today either – especially after what happened last year."

Yuck giggled, remembering what he'd got up to…

Last year, Yuck and Polly had gone swimming at Waterworld with their friends Little Eric and Juicy Lucy. Waterworld was brilliant – it had two water slides that coiled round and down into a big fish-shaped pool.

While Yuck and Little Eric were queuing for the slides, Polly and Lucy barged in.

"We were here first," Polly said.

"No you weren't," Yuck replied.

A lifeguard came over. "Hey, what's all the arguing?" he asked.

"It's Yuck. He shouldn't be allowed on the slides," Polly said. "He can't even swim."

"That's a lie, Polly," Yuck said.

Juicy Lucy turned to the lifeguard, "Little Eric can't swim either," she told him.

"Yes I can," Little Eric said.

The lifeguard frowned at Yuck and Little Eric. "I'm sorry, boys, but if you can't swim you'll have to leave."

Polly and Lucy sniggered as Yuck and Little Eric were made to go back to the changing room and get dressed.

"It's so unfair," Little Eric said, putting his socks and shoes back on. "I love Waterworld and now we're not allowed on the slides."

"We'll get Polly and Lucy back," Yuck said. He whispered a plan to Little Eric, and they set to work. First they went to the vending machine in the lobby. Little Eric bought a can of SUN FIZZ and Yuck bought a CHOCOLOG chocolate bar, then they crept back to the poolside. They watched as Polly and Lucy climbed the steps to the top of the water slides. When the lifeguard wasn't looking, Yuck and Little Eric climbed up after them.

Lucy slid down one slide, and Little Eric poured the SUN FIZZ behind her.

Polly slid down the other slide, and Yuck unwrapped the CHOCOLOG and sent it down after her.

Quickly, Yuck and Little Eric raced to the spectators' area to watch…

As Lucy shot from the end of one slide into the pool, the SUN FIZZ trickled after her, turning the water yellow.

"Wee!" Little Eric called loudly. "Lucy's done a wee in the pool!"

The lifeguard saw the yellow water and blew his whistle. "Young lady, get out at once!" he ordered.

"But—"

"No weeing in the pool!"

Just at that moment, Polly shot from the end of the other slide. The CHOCOLOG came out after her and floated on the surface of the water.

"Poo!" Yuck called loudly. "Polly's done a poo in the pool!"

The lifeguard saw the brown floater and blew his whistle. "Young lady, get out at once!" he ordered.

"But—"

"No pooing in the pool!"

The lifeguard sent Polly and Lucy to get changed, their faces red with embarrassment.

In the kitchen Yuck had finished his Monster Snaps and was slurping the leftover milk from his bowl. If he wasn't allowed to go swimming today, then what else could he do that was fun?

Through the window he saw Dad in the garden, digging. "I know what! Can I play in the garden, Mum?" he asked with milk dribbling down his chin. "That's fun too!"

"Yuck, I've already told you, having fun is NOT a proper New Year's resolution!" Mum said. "So there'll be no playing in the garden today either – not after what happened last year."

Yuck giggled, remembering what he'd got up to…

Last year, Yuck had been in the garden collecting snails. He'd collected a whole bucketful and they were all sliming inside it.

Dad was watering MIRACLE GROW onto his tomato plants to make them grow bigger, and Polly was planting flowers in flowerpots.

"You're revolting, Yuck," Polly said, seeing him place a snail on his hand and letting it slime up his arm.

"But snail slime is brilliant," Yuck replied.

Yuck had an idea — a way to make even more slime. When Dad wasn't looking, he borrowed the bottle of MIRACLE GROW and poured it into his bucket of snails. He left them overnight to stew.

The next morning, when Yuck went to check on the snails, to his delight the MIRACLE GROW had worked — the snails had grown and were now loose in the garden, each as big as a dog!

Polly came to water her flowers and got quite a shock – they'd all been eaten, and so had Dad's tomatoes! A huge snail slimed towards her. "Hey, what's going on?" Polly cried, trying to shoo it away. She slipped in its slime and it slid over her, licking her face. "Urrgh! Get it off me! Get it off me!"

In the kitchen Yuck rummaged in the box of Monster Snaps and pulled out a small toy: a Micro-Monster — one of ten to collect! He stretched its rubber arms. There must be something fun I can do today, he thought. "Mum, it's not good to break a promise, is it?" he asked.

"No, Yuck."

"Well I promised to have fun so—"

"YUCK! HOW MANY MORE TIMES DO I HAVE TO TELL YOU? Promising to have fun is NOT a proper New Year's resolution!"

Polly stepped over and sniggered in Yuck's ear. "Ha ha, no fun for you today!"

Yuck did a Monster Snap burp right in her face.

"PHWOAR!" Polly yelled. "Your breath stinks, Yuck! You haven't cleaned your teeth!"

Polly took her piece of paper from the fridge door. "Yuck, why don't you promise to clean your teeth like me? That's a proper New Year's resolution."

"I'm not sure that's a good idea, Polly," Yuck

I promise to clean my teeth.

replied. "Don't you remember? I cleaned my teeth once last year." He giggled, thinking back to what had happened...

One evening last year, Yuck had been in his room eating a packet of toffee twirls.

Mum called up the stairs, "Don't forget it's the dentist tomorrow, Yuck. Give your teeth a good clean before you go to bed."

Oh, no! Not the dentist! Yuck thought. The Evil Extractor! The Driller Killer!

Polly Princess poked her nose round Yuck's door. "Worried are you, Yuck? I bet you have to have a filling."

A filling! Yuck thought. Aaargh! He imagined the dentist's dreaded drill drilling into his teeth.

Polly grinned a wicked pearly-white grin. "You'll probably have to have an injection too!" she said.

An injection! Yuck thought. No way! Quickly, he leapt from his bed and ran downstairs. From the kitchen cupboard he grabbed a packet of cheese-and-onion crisps and a tube of garlic paste. He took them to the bathroom, locked the door and set to work on a plan. Taking his toothbrush from the rack, Yuck squeezed garlic paste onto its bristles then crushed cheese-and-onion crisps on top. He started brushing. The flavour was so strong that 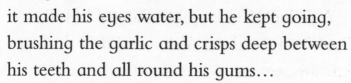 it made his eyes water, but he kept going, brushing the garlic and crisps deep between his teeth and all round his gums…

All that night and all the next morning, Yuck let the flavours stew. He kept his mouth shut, not saying a single word, all the way to the dentist's.

Polly went first to the dentist's chair. A few minutes later she returned grinning. "He said my teeth are perfect. Your turn now, Yuck."

Yuck headed in and lay on the dentist's big chair. The dentist looked down at him. "Good morning, young man. Your sister tells me you need some fillings. She says you haven't been brushing."

Yuck could see right up the dentist's hairy nose. It was time to put his plan into action... As the dentist picked up a syringe ready to give Yuck an injection, Yuck rubbed his tongue along his teeth, dislodging the garlic and the cheese and onion.

"Open wide, Yuck," the dentist said.

Yuck opened his mouth and a cloud of stinky gas rose into the dentist's face.

"Argh!" the dentist cried, his nose curling and his eyes watering.

Mum and Polly came running in to see what the fuss was. "Is everything all right?" Mum asked.

"What's that horrible smell?" Polly asked.

"It's your brother," the dentist said, pointing to Yuck. "His breath honks!" The stench was too strong for the dentist and he staggered across the room, choking. He bumped into Polly, knocking her over. "Ouch!" she cried as the syringe stuck in her bottom!

In the kitchen Yuck pinged the Micro-Monster with his spoon, firing it across the room. It landed in a pile of dough on the kitchen counter.

"Yuck, stop messing about," Mum said. She was making pizza for lunch.

"But I'm bored, Mum. I want to have fun."

Polly was sweeping Monster Snaps from the floor, cleaning up for Mum. "Unlucky, Yuck. You're never going to have any fun again," she sniggered.

Yuck wiggled his toes, releasing the smell of foot cheese. "Phwoar! Your feet stink, Yuck!" Polly cried. "You haven't had a bath! Why don't you promise to have lots of baths like me?"

Yuck wiggled his toes again. "I'm not sure that's a good idea," he said. "Don't you remember, I had a bath once last year." He giggled, thinking back to what had happened…

Last year, Yuck had come home muddy from playing football.

"Yuck, it's bath time," Mum called.

Yuck ran to his room and hid under his bed. He hated having baths.

Polly ran to look for him. "I know you're in here, Yuck," she said, opening the door. She looked behind his desk, then in his wardrobe, then under the bed. She grinned. "Mum, I've found him!"

"Traitor," Yuck said to her.

Mum came in and dragged Yuck out. "Come with me at once you dirty boy. It's time for your bath."

"But, Mum, I'm allergic to baths," Yuck said. "Polly can have my bath instead."

"Polly's going to have one after you," Mum told him, pushing Yuck into the bathroom. As she closed the door, Yuck heard Polly sniggering.

He looked at the bath full of soapy water and sighed. What was the point of having a bath when he'd only get dirty again tomorrow? he thought.

Yuck rolled up his trouser legs and admired his muddy knees. He checked his belly-button for button gunk. It seemed a shame to wash it all away.

He sat on the edge of the bath and
dipped his hand in, splashing the water
noisily, pretending he was washing. "Mmm,
I love baths," he called loudly.

"And don't forget to wash your hair,"
Polly called from the hallway.

But instead Yuck set to work on getting
Polly back for snitching. He prepared a little
surprise for her...

Yuck opened the bottle of shampoo and emptied it down the sink, then from the bathroom cabinet he fetched a tube of hair-removal cream that Mum used on her legs. He squirted the hair-removal cream into the shampoo bottle and placed it back on the side of the bath.

Yuck pulled out the bath plug, letting the clean water run away. "I've finished!" he called. He wrapped himself in towels then opened the door to leave.

"That was quick, Yuck," Mum said.

Yuck rubbed a towel on his head pretending to dry his hair. "It's nice to be clean," he said. "Your turn now Polly."

Polly pushed past Yuck and closed the door behind her.

Yuck heard the taps running as she filled the bath. He listened to the sound of splashing as Polly started scrubbing herself clean. "Don't forget to wash your hair, Polly," he called.

Soon after, there came a scream.

"Polly, is everything OK in there?" Yuck called, giggling.

"My hair!" Polly cried. "My hair's fallen out!"

The bathroom door opened and Polly poked her head out scowling. She was completely bald!

In the kitchen, Yuck dipped his Micro-Monster in a pot of jam, then marched it across the table. It left a trail of Monster prints over Polly's New Year's resolutions.

"Yuck, look what you've done!" she yelled.

"Oops, sorry," Yuck said. He got up and marched the sticky Micro-Monster around the toaster on the counter instead, then over the fruitbowl and across an exercise book.

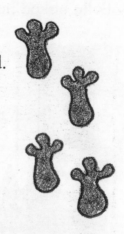

"Not on that! That's my holiday homework!" Polly yelled.

"What holiday homework?"

"Yuck, why don't you promise to do your homework like I have?"

Yuck licked his sticky Micro-Monster. "I'm not sure that's a good idea," he said. "Don't you remember, I did my homework once last year." He giggled, thinking back to what had happened...

The last time Yuck had been set homework, it was to prepare for the end-of-year test. While Polly did hers Yuck read his comic on his bed.

Polly poked her nose round Yuck's door. "Why aren't you working?" she asked.

"Because I'm already too clever," Yuck told her.

"Rubbish," Polly said. "I'm going to get much better marks than you."

She stuck her tongue out then went back to her books to study.

Yuck smiled, and continued with his comic, scratching his head as he read. Hundreds of head lice were looking down from his hair, reading his comic too.

"All set for tomorrow?" he asked them.

"Ready when you are, Yuck," the head lice replied in tiny little voices.

Yuck had a plan: a way to get top marks without doing any homework at all.

The next day, at school, everyone sat at desks in the assembly hall as Mr Reaper the headmaster handed out the test. There were over a hundred questions!

"You have one hour to complete the test, starting now!" the Reaper said.

While everyone worked away in silence, Yuck sent his head lice on their mission. They hopped from head to head along the lines of children.

As each person began writing their answers, the head lice hopped back relaying the information to Yuck. The head lice were so tiny that no one noticed them spying. They queued up behind Yuck's ear, one after another, and whispered the answers to him, "Nine times eleven is ninety-nine... the capital city of France is Paris... the largest mammal is the blue whale."

In no time at all, Yuck had finished the test.

'Nine times eleven is ninety nine'

Yuck looked around to see how Polly was getting on. She was still writing.

"Now, go get her," Yuck whispered to his head lice.

The head lice hopped across the room to Polly. All together, they dived into her hair. and started tugging at it. Yuck saw Polly scratch her head, first with one hand then with the other.

"Ouch, ooh, eek!" she cried.

The Reaper called from the front of the assembly hall. "Silence!"

Polly was scratching frantically. "Aargh, yikes, yowsers!"

The headmaster marched over to her. "I said no talking!"

"But I'm all itchy!" Polly said. "There's something in my hair!"

The Reaper took a closer look and saw Polly's hair crawling with head lice.

"You've got nits!" he told her.

"But I can't have. I didn't this morning," Polly said.

"You're to leave the room immediately, before anyone else catches them," the Reaper told her.

"But I haven't finished the test," Polly said.

"You should have thought about that before you came to school with head lice."

As the Reaper marched Polly away, she passed Yuck's desk.

"Oh dear, Polly," Yuck said. "It looks like I'm the cleverest after all."

In the kitchen Yuck stuffed the Micro-Monster up his nose then pulled it back out dripping in mucous.

"Yuck, that's gross!" Mum said.

"I like doing it. It's fun!" Yuck told her. "Having fun is my New Year's resolution, remember?"

"Right, Yuck, I've had enough of this! Promising to have fun is NOT a proper New Year's resolution. Why can't you think of one like Polly's?"

Yuck looked at the piece of paper with Polly's New Year's resolutions written on it. **I promise to help around the house**, he read.

Yuck had an idea. "OK, Mum, if you insist. This year, I promise to help around the house, and I'm going to start by helping with lunch right now. You and Polly can go and have a rest."

"Really? That's very kind of you, Yuck," Mum said. She went to the living room and Polly followed.

"But Yuck never helps, Mum," Polly said. "What's he up to?"

"Polly, he's trying to be good," Mum told her.

Yuck set to work preparing lunch. Today was going to be extra fun after all, he decided. Mum had already rolled out the pizza base and all it needed now was its topping. What flavour pizza shall we have, he thought?

Yuck covered the pizza base in ketchup then took off his socks. From between his toes he scraped lumps of toe cheese and wiped them on the pizza. Then he picked his toenails and sprinkled the clippings on top like bits of onion. He rolled his trouser leg up, and picked at his grazed knee, peeling off bits of scab like pepperoni. He placed them on top, plus another scab from his elbow. He pulled long stringy bogeys from his nose and laid them on like green peppers, then added lumps of earwax like pineapple chunks.

He popped the pizza in the oven.

When it was ready, Yuck called everyone to the table, "Mum, Polly, Dad, it's time to eat!"

Mum and Polly sat at the table. "Well I must say it's nice of you to help with lunch, Yuck," Mum said, seeing the pizza that Yuck had made.

"Pizza's my favourite!" Polly said.

Dad came in from the garden. "Mmm, that looks nice," he said.

"Yuck made it," Mum explained.

"Yuck did? Really?" Dad looked surprised. "That's very good of you to help, Yuck."

"It's my New Year's resolution," Yuck explained, serving everyone a slice. "Tuck in," he said.

Mum, Dad and Polly each bit into their slices of pizza.

Yuck giggled as they ate. "Do you like it?" he asked.

Mum was chewing on a bogey pepper. "It's quite sticky," she said.

Dad was munching a scab. "It's quite crunchy," he said.

Polly picked a toenail from her lip. "It's…
er…" She was having trouble speaking.
Melted toe cheese was wrapped around her
tongue, sticking her mouth together. "It's
R… R… REVOLTING!"

Yuck smiled. It was still only the first day of the new year and he was already having LOTS of yucky fun. "Happy New Year everyone!"

GET THE GIGGLES WITH ALL YUCK'S BOOKS!

YUCK'S SLIME MONSTER
(and Yuck's Gross Party)

YUCK'S AMAZING UNDERPANTS
(and Yuck's Scary Spider)

YUCK'S PET WORM
(and Yuck's Rotten Joke)

YUCK'S MEGA MAGIC WAND
(and Yuck's Pirate Treasure)

YUCK'S FART CLUB
(and Yuck's Sick Trick)

YUCK'S ALIEN ADVENTURE
(and Yuck's Slobbery Dog)

YUCK'S ABOMINABLE BURP BLASTER
(and Yuck's Remote Control Revenge)

YUCK'S BIG BOGEYS
(and Yuck's Smelly Socks)

YUCK'S SUPERCOOL SNOTMAN
(and Yuck's Dream Machine)

YUCK'S ROBOTIC BOTTOM
(and Yuck's Wild Weekend)

YUCK'S FANTASTIC FOOTBALL MATCH
(and Yuck's Creepy Crawlies)

YUCK'S CRAZY CHRISTMAS
(and Yuck's Naughty New Year)

Join Yuck's fanclub at
YUCKWEB.COM